Monster!

First published in 2009
by Wayland

This paperback edition published in 2010

Text copyright © Anne Rooney 2009
Illustration copyright © Fabiano Fiorin 2009

Wayland
338 Euston Road
London NW1 3BH

Wayland Australia
Level 17/207 Kent Street
Sydney, NSW 2000

Series Editor: Louise John
Editor: Katie Powell
Cover design: Paul Cherrill
Design: D.R.ink
Consultant: Shirley Bickler

A CIP catalogue record for this book is available from the British Library.

ISBN 9780750255448 (hbk)
ISBN 9780750255486 (pbk)

Printed in China

Wayland is a division of Hachette Children's Books,
an Hachette Livre UK Company

www.hachettelivre.co.uk

Monster!

Written by Anne Rooney
Illustrated by Fabiano Fiorin

WAYLAND

"Bedtime, Henry," said Mum. "What are you doing under the bed?"

"Checking for monsters," said Henry.

"There's no such thing as monsters!" said Mum. "Go to sleep."

Henry looked behind the door and in the cupboard. There were no monsters.

9

He sat in the dark. There was something moving under the bed.

"Mum!" shouted Henry.
"There's a monster under
my bed."

Mum turned the light back on.

"There are no such things as monsters!" she said. "Go to sleep, Henry."

Henry tried to go to sleep.
But he could hear a monster
scratching under the bed.

"Dad! There's a monster in here," he shouted.

Dad came in. "There are no such things as monsters!" he said. "Go to sleep, Henry."

In the morning, Kate
helped Henry to make
a 'NO MONSTERS' sign.

Henry put it on his
bedroom door.

"That will keep the monsters
away," said Kate.

But Henry was still scared.

"Monsters are bad," he said. "Maybe they will not read the sign."

The next day, Henry tipped
out his junk box.

He worked all morning.

"What are you making?"
asked Mum.

"It's a monster trap,
of course!" said Henry.

At bedtime, Henry went upstairs without a fuss.

"Aren't you scared of monsters?" asked Kate.
"Not any more!" said Henry.

Henry lay very still. He was sure there was a monster under the bed.

He stayed quiet.

Click! The trap snapped shut!

"Mum!" shouted Henry. "I've got the monster!"

Everyone came to look at the monster under the bed. It was very small!

No Monsters

"Can we keep it, Mum, please?" asked Kate.

"There ARE such things as monsters, after all!" said Henry.

START READING is a series of highly enjoyable books for beginner readers. **The books have been carefully graded to match the Book Bands widely used in schools.** This enables readers to be sure they choose books that match their own reading ability.

Look out for the Band colour on the book in our Start Reading logo.

The Bands are:

Pink Band 1

Red Band 2

Yellow Band 3

Blue Band 4

Green Band 5

Orange Band 6

Turquoise Band 7

Purple Band 8

Gold Band 9

START READING books can be read independently or shared with an adult. They promote the enjoyment of reading through satisfying stories supported by fun illustrations.

Anne Rooney is often bothered by small monsters at home. She lives in a state of chaos with her two daughters, a tortoise called Tor2 and a blue lobster called Marcel.

Fabiano Fiorin lives and works in a magical city, Venice, where there are canals full of sea water instead of roads, and there are boats instead of cars. Fabiano thinks the best thing about being an illustrator is that you can pretend to be the characters you draw and you can have lots of adventures.